Gnomeo & Juliet

THE JUNIOR NOVELIZATION

ISBN: 978-0-7364-2823-1

www.randomhouse.com/kids

Printed in the United States of America

10 9 8 7 6 5 4 3 2

Gnomeo & Juliet

THE JUNIOR NOVELIZATION

Adapted by Molly McGuire Woods

Random House 🏠 New York

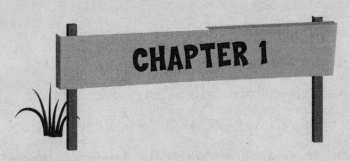

CHAPTER 1

"I'm in love, Benny. Real, passionate, undying, everlasting love," Gnomeo said to his best friend. They were staring down at the shiny lawn mower parked in the corner of Miss Montague's toolshed.

Miss Montague, a human, had already left her house for the day. That meant that the ceramic gnomes, wooden whirligigs, concrete statues, plastic lawn ornaments, and tin weather vanes decorating her prizewinning garden could come to life. They were free to move around only when humans could not see them. Even though Miss Montague would never know it, Gnomeo, Benny, and all the other blue-painted gnomes in her garden took great pride in helping to keep her plants and lawn beautifully trimmed and tidy.

Benny was small, even by gnome standards, but he had a very tall pointed blue hat to make up for his short stature. Like Gnomeo, he loved a fine-tuned, high-horsepower lawn mower. But if there was one thing Gnomeo and Benny loved more than lawn mowers themselves, it was racing them. And today seemed like a good day for Gnomeo to make the red-hatted gnomes in the garden next door eat his blue dust.

"Come on. Let's give those Reds another lesson in how it's done," Gnomeo said.

"We've got to do more than show them how it's done," Benny growled. Just thinking of the Reds made the normally mild-mannered gnome go a little crazy. "We've got to take their cheaply painted faces and grind them into the dirt. Grab them by their red hats and smash them against a wall over and over and over—"

"Whoa," Gnomeo said, whacking Benny on the hat to snap him out of his sudden tirade. "Let's go before Mom puts us to work. Shroom, are we all clear?"

A small blue-capped stone mushroom nodded from his lookout position by the door. Gnomeo pushed the lawn mower out of the shed and into the sunlight.

"The wheelbarrow is in the garden," Benny whispered nervously as Gnomeo's mother, Lady Bluebury, approached. "The pigeon has landed. *The pigeon has landed.* YOUR MOM IS COMING THIS WAY!"

"What?" Gnomeo asked. "Why didn't you just say that?"

"I was speaking in code," Benny replied sheepishly.

"Don't worry. Just get this to the alley," Gnomeo said, pointing at the lawn mower. "I'll catch up with you later."

Benny started to move the mower as Gnomeo and Shroom ran off to intercept Lady Bluebury.

"Mom!" Gnomeo cried out merrily, grabbing her arm and leading her away from the shed. "Have you ever seen our beautiful garden from this angle?"

"Oh yes. Beautiful. Especially the wisteria," Lady Bluebury replied. "So serene. So majestic—"

"So dignified," Gnomeo added in his most earnest tone as he gazed upon the wisteria.

The pretty flowering tree was planted in an old toilet bowl. Miss Montague thought the toilet gave her garden just the right touch of whimsy.

"That wisteria tree was your father's pride and joy," Lady Bluebury said with a distant sigh. "May he rest in pieces."

Gnomeo put his arm around his mother and gave her a gentle hug.

"You remind me so much of him," Lady Bluebury continued. Then she looked into her son's face and smiled mischievously. "Which is why I want you to go out there and show those blooming Reds who's *really* the best!"

Gnomeo was confused for a moment, and then a wide grin spread across his face. Lady Bluebury became serious again, and she waved her son away as though she had more important business to attend to somewhere else in the garden.

Gnomeo ran toward the gate that led to the back alley—and the race—as fast as he could.

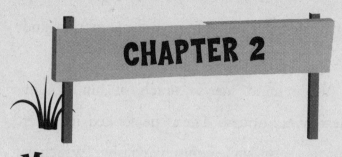

CHAPTER 2

Miss Montague's next-door neighbor was named Mr. Capulet. He was also a gardener. He liked to decorate his garden with gnomes wearing red hats in the same way that Miss Montague liked to beautify her garden with gnomes in blue hats. Like Miss Montague, Mr. Capulet had no clue that his garden gnomes and lawn ornaments came to life when he was not around. In fact, the friendly competition between the two humans to have the best garden in their little town, Stratford-Upon-Avon, was, in its way, the source of the heated rivalry between the two groups of gnomes. Over the years, it had become Blues against Reds, and Reds against Blues. Every gnome on each side played his or her part . . . even the pretty daughter of Lord Redbrick, the leader of the red gnomes.

"Wow! A Cupid's Arrow orchid!" Juliet exclaimed. She had just climbed a tree to get a better look at the flower growing out of the top of a neglected greenhouse. The derelict greenhouse was situated in an abandoned garden opposite the Montague and Capulet gardens.

"Juliet," croaked a frog-shaped fountain named Nanette. "Come down from there! What if your dad sees you?"

As if on cue, the girls heard a booming voice.

"*Aaaargh! Juuu-liiiii-et!*" shouted Lord Redbrick.

Hearing her father's call, Juliet jumped. She lost her footing on the tree branch, and her toe sent a red apple flying. It crashed into a ceramic planter on the ground at Lord Redbrick's feet. Juliet grasped another branch and swung through the air. She landed gracefully right on the spot where the planter had shattered.

"Hi, Dad," she said casually.

"Juliet! Do you want to get smashed to bits?" Lord Redbrick scolded her. He worried about his only daughter, wanting to keep her safe and sound in the garden. Unfortunately, Juliet's love of adventure made for constant tension between them.

"But, Dad, that orchid will put the Blue garden to shame," Juliet said excitedly. "I could get it. It's just across the alley—"

"This feud is none of your consternation," Lord Redbrick interrupted. He liked to use big words, but he didn't always use them correctly.

"Yes, it is," Juliet replied. "I *am* a Red, after all."

Lord Redbrick smiled tenderly at Juliet and said, "Oh, honestly, you are just as impulsivated as your mother." Lord Redbrick stared off into space for a moment, remembering Juliet's mother, who had gotten smashed in a gardening accident long ago. But before Juliet could take advantage of her father's change in sentiment, he added, "Now, back where you belong."

"I can't just stay tucked away on that pedestal all the time," Juliet complained, reluctantly returning to her pedestal in the center of a lush green grotto that Mr. Capulet had lovingly made by hand.

"Going into that alley, you could chip yourself!" Lord Redbrick continued as though he hadn't heard her. "Or worse!"

"So what if I got a little chipped?" Juliet replied. It just wasn't fair! She loved her father, but she hated his rules. Sometimes she felt trapped in the Red garden.

"Mark my words, young lady. You get a chip now, you'll regret it when you're older! Just look at all my scratches and chips!" Lord Redbrick pointed to his arms and legs. They were covered with dents and dings from a lifetime of garden mishaps.

"But I *like* your scratches and chips, Dad! They're you!" Juliet replied. To her, Lord Redbrick's scarred exterior meant that he had been somewhere and done something exciting.

"Well, they are not *you!*" Lord Redbrick exclaimed, exasperated. "When will you realize that you're delicate?"

"I'm not delicate!" Juliet cried out, frustrated.

"She's *definitely* not delicate," Nanette the frog chimed in.

"Stubborn girl," Lord Redbrick muttered as he walked away. As far as he was concerned, the conversation was over.

"I'll show him who's delicate," Juliet said under her breath. She looked up at the Cupid's Arrow orchid growing through the roof of the old greenhouse, and a smile crossed her face.

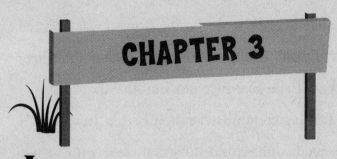

CHAPTER 3

At the same time that Juliet was eyeing the orchid for the Red garden, Gnomeo was getting ready for a lawn mower race in the alley. While Benny and Shroom made the final adjustments to the Blue lawn mower, Gnomeo stole a glance at his competition.

Tybalt was a tough-looking gnome who, much to his embarrassment, had a colorful flower painted on his broad chest. Gnomeo knew he would have to be careful with Tybalt. While most of the gnomes took the rivalry between their two gardens seriously, they didn't really want to see anyone—or any gnome—get hurt. But Tybalt was a bully who longed for nothing more than to win

15

to make himself look good. Gnomeo was positive that Tybalt would resort to all manner of dirty trickery to be sure he came out ahead.

Tybalt's crew wasn't much better. Fawn was a doe-eyed, dim-witted concrete deer who would do anything Tybalt told him to do. He was the bully's biggest fan. There was also a gang of small bargain-basement gnomes collectively known as the goons who hung around Tybalt constantly. And at the moment, they were crawling all over Tybalt's shiny red lawn mower, making sure it was ready to race.

By the time Gnomeo and Tybalt pulled their lawn mowers up to the starting line, a large crowd had gathered to watch.

"*Tybalt, go! Tybalt, go! Tybalt, go!*" the Reds chanted.

"*Gnomeo! Gnomeo! Gnomeo!*" the Blues chanted back loudly.

Gnomeo revved his engine. He had to win this race!

Tybalt sat atop his mower, soaking in the cheers of the screaming Red crowd. "Still stuck with your dad's old rattletrap!" he taunted Gnomeo.

Gnomeo stared Tybalt in the eye but refused to rise to the bait. "Start us up, Dolly!" he called to a pretty girl gnome.

Dolly stood in front of the two mowers. She raised a black-and-white-checkered flag high above her head. She shouted over the roaring engines, "To the end of the alley and back. Your garden's pride is at stake. You know the rules: no hitting, no clipping, no trucking, no busting, no pruning, no flirting, no belching, and *no* cheating!"

"No cheating?" Fawn asked. "That's not fair."

Dolly finished, "On your marks . . . get set—"

"Sucker!" Tybalt yelled, slamming his foot on the gas before Dolly said "go." He took off down the alley, leaving Gnomeo in his wake.

"Go! Go! Go!" Dolly shouted.

Gnomeo cranked his mower into gear and roared down the alleyway. He leaned over his steering wheel in concentration, driving his mower faster and faster until he was almost even with Tybalt. But the big Red gnome swerved in front of him and pulled the mower's release lever, spraying Gnomeo with grass cuttings.

Before Tybalt could enjoy his moment of foul play, Gnomeo sped ahead of him. The Blue gnomes cheered and danced with excitement.

Tybalt pulled another lever on his mower, giving himself a turbo-boost. He bumped Gnomeo from behind, sending the blue-hatted gnome careening toward the fence.

Gnomeo spied a pile of trash ahead and got an idea. He accelerated and aimed right for the garbage. Using the trash pile as a ramp, he shot into the air. The crowd went wild!

But Tybalt wasn't about to give up so easily—even if he had to cheat. The red-hatted gnome reached for a broken pipe in the pile of trash and hurled it at Gnomeo's flying lawn mower.

Clank! The pipe hit Gnomeo's mower, sending it out of control.

Ka-thunk! The mower landed with the dull sound of metal on concrete before bouncing out into the street. Gnomeo was thrown clear, landing safely in an old tire.

Tybalt drove a victory lap around Gnomeo, giving his defeated rival a smug grin. Then he headed toward the finish line.

Before Gnomeo could make another move, a skateboarder zipped past the end of the alley and Gnomeo had to dive for cover so the human wouldn't see him. As soon as the coast was clear, he ran to salvage his lawn mower, only to see—*CRUNCH!*—his prized mower mowed down by a speeding car. The lawn mower bounced back into the alley as a crumpled, ruined heap of metal.

Tybalt skidded to a halt on the winning side of the finish line. Fawn, the goons, and several Reds surrounded him, all cheering wildly.

"You're the greatest, boss!" shouted Fawn.

"Oh, please, please, my friends. Tell me something I don't already know," Tybalt replied, loving all the praise he was receiving.

Benny charged up the alley, waving his arms angrily. "A cheat, a cheat! That's what you are!" he shouted at Tybalt.

Tybalt turned toward Benny. "Well, Benny, I didn't think it was possible, but that mouth of yours is getting even bigger than your hat!" he growled. Then he kicked Benny to the ground!

Gnomeo stormed over, clenching his fists, ready to defend his friend. "Tybalt! You just crossed a line!" he thundered.

"Yeah, the *finish* line!" Tybalt replied with an arrogant laugh. "Adios, loser!"

At a wave of Tybalt's hand, Fawn and the goons started pushing the mower back toward the Red garden. Gnomeo fumed as he watched them disappear through the garden gate.

Benny raced after Tybalt. "Come on out and fight like a gnome!" he yelled.

Gnomeo scowled. Tybalt hadn't deserved to win that race any more than Benny deserved to be treated so meanly.

Gnomeo knew that the Blues would expect him to uphold the honor of their garden. And for that he was going to need Benny's help.

"Well, if he won't come *out*," Gnomeo said, lowering his voice and giving Benny a sly grin, "I guess we'll just have to go *in*."

"Go in? *There?*" Benny gasped. "No Blue has *ever* gone in there."

"Then *I* say it's about time someone did," Gnomeo replied. "And payback is going to be fun."

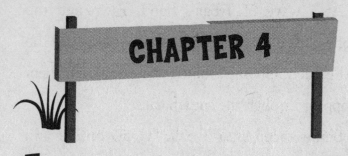

CHAPTER 4

That night, Gnomeo and Shroom met inside the Blue garden's toolshed. They went over their plan to get revenge on Tybalt. They assembled the tools they would need and strapped on their weapons.

Gnomeo was dressed in camouflage from head to toe. He looked into a mirror to check his outfit. Perfect.

Shroom shook his head nervously. No amount of camouflage could make him feel better about this plan. Breaking into the Red garden was serious business!

Gnomeo turned to Shroom. "This mission into Red garden territory is going to require maximum stealth," he said.

"Well, you won't get much stealthier than this," Benny replied, spreading his arms wide as he stepped into the light. *"Hello!"*

Gnomeo was shocked. Benny was disguised as a big, bright yellow flower. He looked ridiculous! He also had a can of spray paint slung over his shoulder that clanked whenever he moved.

This is going to be a long night, Gnomeo thought, shaking his head.

Across the fence in the Red garden, Juliet was making plans of her own. She tiptoed through the darkness toward the garden's back gate. She carefully slipped through the shadows to avoid the rotating searchlight that swept its beam over the ground from a tall ornamental lighthouse.

As she sneaked behind a sleeping fishing gnome, the line on his fishing pole went taut.

Juliet quietly pulled on the line—and discovered a stone fish at the end of it. She quickly lifted the fish off the line.

"Swim away. Be free," Juliet whispered.

"Thank you," replied the stone fish, before its weight caused it to sink straight to the bottom of the pond. "Oh," burbled the fish from under the water.

Juliet took the sleeping gnome's fishing pole and sprinted the rest of the way to the garden gate. She used the fishing line to undo the latch. Silently, she peered across the dark alley at the greenhouse. The orchid was still there.

"All this for a daffy flower?" Nanette's voice cut through the darkness. Juliet shushed her but was relieved that it was just her best friend.

"Yes, and I'm going to need you to cover for me, Nanette," Juliet said, locking eyes with her friend. She hoped Nanette could see how important this was to her. "If my dad asks, just tell him I'm washing my hair."

Nanette looked confused but agreed to do it. She practiced the lines, saying to herself, "I'm washing my hair. I'm washing my hair—"

"No. *I'm* washing *my* hair," Juliet said, then sighed and gave up.

Juliet opened the gate and peeked into the alley. *Grrrrr!* She came face to face with a growling bulldog!

"*Aaaaahh!*" Juliet jumped back into the garden, narrowly missing being bitten. "I'm too easy to see. I need some kind of disguise," she said, thinking out loud.

Nanette's eyes lit up. She loved a good wardrobe challenge. "Oh, a new outfit! I'm on it," she replied, heading for the clothesline.

Juliet peered cautiously into the alley once more. It was all clear now.

Nanette returned a few moments later, looking excited. She threw a bright pink sock with green polka dots over Juliet's head. "Here! Now, *that* is cute!" she cried.

Juliet looked down at her disguise. Anyone would see her coming a mile away in this thing! "Er . . . maybe something a tad less fluorescent pink?" she suggested.

"How much less?" Nanette asked, resting a finger on her chin as she considered the options.

"Try black," Juliet said.

Nanette huffed off to the clothesline again, in search of something less bold. She tugged a black sock off the line and returned to Juliet.

"Trust me," Nanette said. "Nobody is going to pay you any attention in this."

She handed the sock to Juliet.

"Then it's perfect," Juliet replied.

Juliet pulled the disguise over her head and quickly made holes for her arms, legs, and face. She twirled once to show off her handiwork, then gave a kung fu kick for good measure.

"I'm going in," Juliet whispered as she slipped away into the darkness.

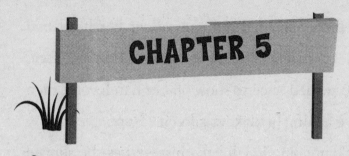

CHAPTER 5

Gnomeo inched his way up to the top of the fence and peeked into the Red garden below. His plan for payback was under way.

He saw Fawn and the other members of Tybalt's gang of goons playing cards. Tybalt was asleep in a bucket hanging over a wishing well.

Good, thought Gnomeo. *They won't notice me.* He hurled the nozzle end of a garden hose over the fence like a rope.

Scrutinizing the Red garden, Gnomeo spotted a motion detector. He also noted the searchlight that continually scanned the yard. He realized that he would have to time things exactly right.

Just then, he heard a loud clanking below him.

He looked down and saw Benny climbing the fence, his paint can clattering behind him. Gnomeo rolled his eyes.

"Shhhh," Gnomeo warned. "Keep quiet."

Gnomeo and Benny worked their way over the top of the fence. They grabbed hold of the long hose's nozzle and held on tight. Gnomeo gave a thumbs-up to Shroom and some stone bunnies in the Blue garden. The bunnies set to work unwinding the long hose reel, slowly lowering Gnomeo and Benny into the Red garden.

Gnomeo felt as if he were in an action movie. *Awesome!* He landed softly on the ground. Benny landed with an awkward *clank* behind him. They made their way toward the garden shed.

Gnomeo and Benny hid behind a large plant and peered out into the yard. Fawn and the goons were still talking at the card table. Now was the time to make a move.

Gnomeo and Benny dashed across the lawn. They made it safely to the shed and grinned at each other. *Success!*

Gnomeo flung open the shed door. Tybalt's shiny red mower sat inside. "Ha ha!" Gnomeo exclaimed. They had come for revenge, and they were about to get it. "Benny, give me the paint."

Gnomeo reached behind him to grab the paint can from his friend. Only . . . Benny wasn't there. "Benny?" Gnomeo whispered.

Gnomeo turned and watched in horror as Benny sprayed graffiti on the Reds' prized wishing well—the one that Tybalt was sleeping above! Benny had abandoned their plan—he'd gone rogue! Gnomeo tried to keep his cool.

Benny shook the can and continued spraying. Tybalt grunted and rolled over, still sleeping soundly in the well's bucket. This was a recipe for disaster.

"Benny! Benny!" Gnomeo whispered.

The tiny gnome didn't stop. His thirst for revenge had taken over. He kept spraying the well with paint. He shook the can again, but he shook it so hard that he lost his grip.

Gnomeo watched as the can flew through the air. It couldn't have been aimed better to set off the motion sensor!

"*Noooo!*" Gnomeo cried. He leaped and caught the can, but it was too late. The motion sensor's alarm went off!

"*Tybalt!*" Lord Redbrick thundered as he came storming across the lawn to see what the noise was all about.

Tybalt jolted awake from his nap. He tumbled out of his bucket and saw Gnomeo.

"Get them, you idiots!" Tybalt called to Fawn and the goons.

"Run for it!" Gnomeo cried. He rolled the

paint can toward Tybalt's goons. They all toppled over, except for Fawn. The deer nimbly hurdled the can and galloped toward Gnomeo and Benny. Thinking fast, Gnomeo pulled some acorns from his belt. He threw them at the ground in front of Fawn. Fawn stumbled and fell.

Gnomeo and Benny dove behind a bush, hiding from Tybalt's gaze.

"Where did he go?" Tybalt asked, looking around the yard. He didn't appreciate being made to look like a fool.

"He's in the begonias," one of the goons replied.

Tybalt gave the goon a cold stare. "Well . . . ," he began. "Do I look like a begonia? Find him!"

Tybalt's crew sprang into action, searching every bush.

"Not here," said one goon.

"Not here, either," echoed Fawn.

Another goon moved toward the bush that

Benny and Gnomeo were hiding behind. Benny stood still, trying to blend in. Gnomeo crouched down behind him. This was it! They were finished!

The goon pulled apart the branches, but all he noticed was a big yellow flower. "Nothing but daisies here," he said.

Gnomeo and Benny glanced at each other in disbelief. Benny's flower costume had worked!

"Come on!" Gnomeo whispered to Benny. They raced for the fence and tugged on the hose's nozzle. On the other side, Shroom and the stone bunnies began to reel in the hose. Gnomeo and Benny were slowly lifted back to the top of the fence.

But just before they would have been safely out of reach, Fawn and the goons saw them and grabbed hold of Gnomeo's foot! Gnomeo tried to shake them off, but it was no use.

Gnomeo had to think of something. "Hold on!" he called to Shroom and the bunnies. Then he pressed the trigger on the hose's nozzle with all his might. Water blasted from the hose, sending them all whipping through the air. But the goons held on tight.

There was only one way out of this, Gnomeo realized. He looked up at Benny. "See you on the other side," he said.

Gnomeo let go of the hose. He and the goons fell to the ground.

"Gnomeo! *Noooo!*" Benny shouted as he left his best friend behind. The stone bunnies quickly pulled Benny to the top of the fence.

Gnomeo landed in a red rowboat planter. Tybalt jumped in front of him. He was holding a trowel as a weapon. Gnomeo grabbed a nearby bamboo pole and prepared to battle. The two gnomes charged at each other. Their makeshift swords clashed.

Suddenly, the lights in Mr. Capulet's house came on.

Gnomeo and Tybalt froze.

Mr. Capulet peered out into the yard. Seeing that his garden was quiet and peaceful, he turned away and switched off the lights.

Gnomeo had a split second to act. He grabbed the clothesline and, pulling back on it, launched himself into the air. Using a piece of clothing from the line as a parachute, he drifted into the sky and over the fence.

"Arghhh!" Tybalt cried, throwing his trowel to the ground.

Gnomeo gave a little wave to Tybalt and his goons.

"I wish I could stay, but . . . gotta fly!" Gnomeo said as he disappeared into the night.

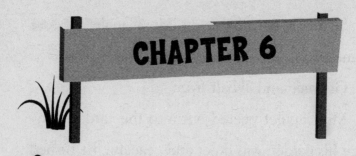

CHAPTER 6

Gnomeo drifted through the sky with his improvised parachute. He made his landing in the overgrown garden across the alley. *What is this place?* he thought. *It sure is quiet . . . and weird.*

Suddenly, he caught a glimpse of something out of the corner of his eye. Looking up, he watched as another gnome in a black costume ran along the garden wall, ducking under tree branches in her way. *Who is that?* Gnomeo wondered. Even in an old black sock, she was beautiful.

Still in his camouflage, Gnomeo followed her, working his way through the overgrown garden. It looked as if she was headed for the old glass greenhouse. A single white orchid was growing out of a hole in the roof of the run-down building.

Juliet pulled herself up to the top of the dilapidated greenhouse. *Whew!* she thought. *I made it!*

Gnomeo sneaked around and scaled a wall on the other side. He reached the rooftop just as Juliet did.

Gnomeo and Juliet locked eyes. Suddenly, it was as if the whole world had stopped just for them. It was love at first sight!

Gnomeo felt dizzy.

Juliet looked as if she might faint.

Gnomeo took a step forward.

Juliet took a step backward.

Both gnomes held their breath.

The spell was broken when they heard a loud *crack!* The glass roof under Juliet's feet began to fracture. She was going to fall!

Gnomeo grabbed her hand just in time. He

pulled with all his might, and the beautiful, mysterious gnome stumbled into his arms.

"Ummm," she said nervously. "You're probably wondering what I'm doing on the roof of your greenhouse. It's just . . . I . . . well, I thought no one lived here."

"Oh . . . this isn't *my* garden," Gnomeo replied.

Juliet laughed. "Oh! Well, that's good. Because I just came to get that orchid." She pointed to the beautiful white bloom curling up through the hole in the roof.

"Oh, this?" Gnomeo asked. He snapped off the orchid and took a sniff. "I don't know," he said. "I think I'm going to have to keep ahold of this one."

"What?" Juliet cried. "But I saw it first. So why don't you just hand it over?" She tried to snatch the flower from Gnomeo.

Gnomeo playfully tossed it from one hand to another. "Well, I grabbed it first," he said, teasing her. "And possession is nine-tenths of the law. But if you want it, come and get it."

"All right," Juliet said. Two could play at this game. She stomped on one of the greenhouse's panes of glass, sending it spinning. It knocked the orchid right out of Gnomeo's hand and into hers.

"Thanks," Juliet said sweetly.

Then Juliet slipped! She dropped the orchid and fell through the hole in the roof. She landed unhurt on a sprinkler pipe inside the greenhouse.

Gnomeo looked down at her from the roof. He was now holding the orchid. "Nice greenhouse, huh?" he said with a smirk.

"Oh yeah, you should see it from here," Juliet called up. She yanked Gnomeo's leg and pulled him into the greenhouse with her. Now the orchid was hers again!

Gnomeo snatched it back. "Who's your gnomie?" he said.

Back and forth they went, taking the orchid from each other.

They made their way down to the floor of the greenhouse, but Gnomeo got out the door first, clutching the orchid. In the garden, he started to run across a log stretched over a pond like a bridge. He was halfway across the log when he noticed that the girl was no longer there. And then, sneaking up on him from behind, she grabbed the flower.

But suddenly the log gave way. *Snap!*

They both plunged into the pond! Juliet's sock and Gnomeo's camouflage came away in the water.

Gnomeo and Juliet looked at each other underwater. For the first time, each noticed the color of the other's hat.

Oh.

No.

Red and blue! This was bad. They were sworn enemies! If anyone saw them together, it would mean major trouble!

Juliet climbed out of the pond, gasping and dripping wet. Her father would never forgive her if she started spending time with a Blue. She hurried toward the alley.

Gnomeo followed her. He had to convince her that they could work things out.

Juliet leaped through a hole in the fence and landed in the alley. She stood—and ran smack into Tybalt, Fawn, and the goons.

"Juliet!" Tybalt exclaimed. "What are you doing out here?"

Juliet paused for a moment. "I'm . . . umm— well, I could ask you the same question, Tybalt," she said cleverly.

"We're looking for a Blue gnome," Tybalt growled. "He's an ugly little fella."

"And his name's Gnomeo," Fawn added.

At the sound of his name, Gnomeo flattened himself against the other side of the fence. He held his breath. Now was not the time to get caught—he had just met the gnome of his dreams!

"You haven't seen him, have you?" Tybalt asked.

Gnomeo stood still, listening carefully. *What will she do?*

"Hmmm." Juliet pretended to think. "He sounds awful! No, I certainly haven't seen him, haven't seen him at all," she said.

"Lucky you," Tybalt snarled. He put his hand on Juliet's arm. "Come on, let's get inside."

Juliet had no choice. She glanced over her shoulder, searching for Gnomeo. She saw him peeping around the overgrown garden's fence.

They locked eyes one last time. Then Juliet disappeared into the Red garden.

Gnomeo was left alone in the empty alley.

"Juliet," he whispered. And then he groaned.

Of all things, why did she have to be a Red?
he thought.

CHAPTER 7

Back in the safety of the Red garden, Nanette was dying for details of Juliet's night.

"So . . . where's this oh-so-important, life-changing orchid?" Nanette asked. It hadn't escaped her that Juliet had sneaked out of the garden for the precious flower but had come back empty-handed.

Juliet didn't answer. She was off in her own world, thinking about Gnomeo. "Um, what orchid?" she said dreamily. She walked up the steps of the grotto.

"Hmmm," Nanette replied. The frog quickly grew suspicious. Juliet was hiding something, she was positive. But what could it be? She caught up with Juliet and grabbed her by the shoulders.

"What?" Juliet asked.

Nanette looked deep into Juliet's eyes. She knew her friend better than anyone. If Juliet had a secret, Nanette would figure it out. Then, all of a sudden, she had it!

"No way!" Nanette exclaimed. "*You* met a *boy*," she declared, pointing a finger at Juliet.

Juliet looked flustered. "What? No!" she cried. "Well, maybe . . . sort of . . . I'm . . ." Juliet blushed. She couldn't hold it in any longer. "*Yes!* Yes, I did!" she shouted. It felt great to tell someone.

Nanette shook Juliet giddily. "I need details, and *go slowly*. Is he totally gorgeous?" she asked.

"*Totally*," Juliet gushed.

"Does he have a nice round belly?" Nanette inquired.

"Well, let's just call it sturdy," Juliet replied.

Nanette whistled. This gnome sounded too good to be true!

But Juliet knew she had to tell Nanette the

whole truth about Gnomeo. He was a Blue and she was a Red. And that meant they could never be together.

Juliet tried to think of the right words to make Nanette understand. "His hat . . . ," she started. "You know, I suppose, in a certain light, you might say it looks sort of . . . blue."

"*Blue*," Nanette repeated. It wasn't quite a question and it wasn't quite a statement. Then she became silent, which was hard for Nanette to do. Juliet *had* to be kidding. Nanette laughed nervously. "Oh, this is one of your little jokes. Ahahaha. Ha ha. Ha ha!"

Juliet gave Nanette a serious look. She wasn't joking.

"Oh, flippin', flamin' Nora! She's smooching the face off a Blue!" Nanette exclaimed. This was juicier gossip than she'd thought!

Juliet clamped her hand over Nanette's mouth.

The last thing she needed was for this news to get out. "Shhh—please shush, Nanette. Just zip it," Juliet said, making a "zip your lips" motion across her mouth with her finger.

Nanette did the same. "*Zzzzip,*" she said. Juliet's secret was safe with her. But she was too excited about it to keep quiet. "Oh, Juliet! This is fantastic!"

Juliet looked at her friend hopefully. If Nanette really thought it was okay, maybe it was. "Is it?" she asked.

"It's doomed!" Nanette cried. "*Doomed!*"

"What?" Juliet said.

"A Red and a Blue. It just can't be! It's a *doomed* love, and that's the best kind!" Nanette explained. "You'll never see him again! And then, one day, when you die, you'll be all, 'Oh, my true love, I only saw him once! Oh! Oh, ohhhh . . . !'" Nanette pretended to faint in Juliet's arms.

Shocked, Juliet dropped Nanette. "I'll only see him once? What do you mean I'll only see him once?" she exclaimed.

But Nanette was lost in her own daydream now. "How romantically tragic!" she cried, swooning again.

Juliet bit her lip. She couldn't bear it if Nanette was right.

Nanette picked a flower. She began to pluck its petals off one by one, singing, "Your love is doomed." *Pluck!* "Your love is dead." *Pluck!* "Your love is doomed." *Pluck!* "Your love is dead." *Pluck! Pluck! Pluck!*

Nanette wandered off, leaving Juliet alone with her thoughts.

Juliet heaved a big sigh. *Blue.* She had finally met her perfect match, and he was out of reach. But maybe—

"Doomed!" Nanette cried out in the darkness.

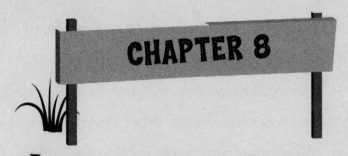

CHAPTER 8

As Juliet continued to worry, Gnomeo was busy making plans to see her again. He sneaked quietly through the back gate into the Red garden. As he slipped stealthily along the fence, he overheard a conversation between two gnomes.

"I've never seen Lord Redbrick so riled up! We have to find Gnomeo," one gnome said to the other. They moved away and joined a large group of Reds by the wishing well. They were inspecting the Blue graffiti Benny had left behind.

Gnomeo took a deep breath and continued his search for Juliet.

Finally, he spotted her high on her balcony at the center of the grotto. She looked beautiful in the moonlight. It sounded as if she was talking to herself. Gnomeo listened.

"Oh, Gnomeo, Gnomeo, are we really doomed, Gnomeo, to never see each other again?" Juliet cried. "Why must you wear a blue hat? Why couldn't it be red, or green, or purple? Because you're a Blue, my father sees red. Because I'm a Red, I'm feeling blue. That shouldn't be the thing to keep us apart, should it?"

Gnomeo couldn't believe his ears. Juliet was talking about *him*! He couldn't resist letting her know he had heard her. "No! No! It shouldn't! I couldn't have said it better myself!" he called out.

Juliet jumped at the sound of another voice. She was alone, wasn't she? Then she saw Gnomeo standing below. Her cheeks flushed as red as her hat. "Oh," she said, collecting herself. "Did you just hear all of that? What are you doing here?"

"I don't know," Gnomeo replied, suddenly

feeling shy. "I . . . umm . . . I came here to . . . well, I just wanted to see you again."

Juliet's heart melted. But then she nervously looked around. She began to panic. "Are you crazy?" she asked. "If Dad finds you here, he'll bury you under the patio!"

Gnomeo waved his hand at the mention of Lord Redbrick. Juliet's father scared the paint off him, but Gnomeo didn't want Juliet to think he was a wimp. He strolled casually toward her—and tripped over a rock. *Oooff. So much for smooth,* he thought.

Unfortunately, Gnomeo's foot had landed on the switch that controlled Mr. Capulet's mechanized grotto display. Before Gnomeo and Juliet could do anything to stop it, the garden lit up with lights and blaring music—and Juliet's balcony started to spin. Her grotto now looked and sounded like a wild nightclub!

"*Ahhh!* Quick, turn . . . it . . . off!" Juliet yelled over the noise.

Gnomeo tried everything he could think of to stop the earsplitting music. Nothing worked! "The button's stuck!" he called.

Across the garden, Lord Redbrick raised his head. What was all that noise? He marched in the direction of the music.

"Juliet!" he hollered.

As Gnomeo continued to struggle with the switch and wires, Shroom suddenly appeared. Benny had sent him into the Red garden to find Gnomeo.

Juliet spotted Lord Redbrick headed right for them.

"My dad's coming!" she warned Gnomeo.

Just then, Nanette hopped over to investigate the noise. "Juliet! What's with the—" she started, but Shroom tripped over some wires and landed right in her mouth! She removed Shroom and then spotted Gnomeo. "So," she said, turning to him. "You must be Gnomeo. Lovely to meet you in the thirty seconds before you're discovered and killed."

Nanette sat down on a nearby rock. She wanted a good seat for all the action. She knew that Gnomeo and Juliet were doomed, but she hadn't expected their love affair to come to an end quite so soon!

Juliet waved at Gnomeo frantically. "Quick! Hide!" she cried.

Gnomeo grabbed Shroom, dove into the garden pond, and held his breath.

Lord Redbrick stomped through Juliet's grotto. He reached behind a flowerpot and pulled a plug from a socket hidden there. The lights snapped off and the music went silent.

"Juliet! I've told you before—no music in the

grotto after ten o'clock. What's going on here?" her father demanded.

"It was a . . . I saw a . . . a squirrel . . . and he . . . ," Juliet said, struggling to come up with an excuse—one that wouldn't give Gnomeo away.

Luckily, Lord Redbrick was too flustered by the night's events to be very worried about Juliet's explanation. "Well, okay. But no mucking about, especially tonight," he told her. "We've been attacked. By a Blue!"

Nanette and Juliet eyed each other.

"And if I ever get my hands on that Blue"— Lord Redbrick clenched his fists—"he'll be sleeping with the fishes!"

Just then, Gnomeo popped out of the water, gasping for breath.

At the sound of Gnomeo's splashing, Lord Redbrick turned around.

Nanette leaped in front of Lord Redbrick

just in time, blocking his view of the pond—and Gnomeo. "Lord Redbrick!" she called, and started asking him silly questions to distract him.

Gnomeo saw his opportunity to get Juliet's attention. "I guess now isn't the best time to talk?" he whispered.

"It's not ideal," Juliet whispered back. She looked nervously toward her father.

"But I—" Gnomeo started again. He wanted to tell Juliet how he felt about her, but he wasn't sure where to begin.

"Just go! Please go," Juliet begged him. She cared too much about him to see him get caught.

"But I just came here to tell you I . . . um, I—" Gnomeo tried again.

"What? You what?" Juliet asked. Then she heard her father approaching again. "Sorry," she said quickly. She pushed Gnomeo back under the pond water and turned toward her dad.

"Juliet, is there something wrong with the pond?" Lord Redbrick asked.

"The pond? No, it's fine. Just as pondy as ever—ha ha," she said, laughing nervously. Then she pointed over her dad's shoulder. "Oh my gosh! What is that thing over there?"

Lord Redbrick turned away from the pond. "What? What is it?" he asked.

Juliet motioned to Nanette.

Nanette pulled Gnomeo and Shroom out of the pond and pushed them toward the gate. "Okay. Bye-bye, then. Good night, sweet prince. Parting is such sweet sorrow," she said quickly.

Nanette shoved Gnomeo and Shroom out into the alley and slammed the garden gate behind them. She wiped the sweat from her brow. *That was close!*

Shroom gave a consoling whimper as he followed Gnomeo down the alley. Gnomeo was feeling sorry for himself. He had been so close to telling Juliet his true feelings for her—but the timing, not to mention the whole situation, was less than perfect. He paused in front of the deserted garden where he'd first met Juliet. He looked toward the greenhouse. Then he got an idea.

Juliet ran over to Nanette. "Nanette, where's Gnomeo? Has he gone?" she asked. She clutched Nanette's arm.

"Yep. Gone forever," Nanette informed her friend.

Juliet looked devastated. "What?" she cried. She climbed toward the top of the fence, hoping for one last glimpse of Gnomeo through the wooden slats of the trellis that extended along the fence's edge.

When she reached the top of the fence, she unexpectedly came face to face with Gnomeo, who was staring through the slats in the trellis, hoping to get one last glimpse of her! In his hand he held the white orchid that Juliet loved so much.

"I think you'll find this does actually belong to you," Gnomeo said.

Juliet smiled shyly as she took the flower. "Thank you," she said, blushing.

They stared into each other's eyes. But Juliet knew that they couldn't be together. She started to leave, but Gnomeo stopped her.

"I can't go," he said.

"I know how you feel," she replied.

"No, really . . . I can't go. I'm stuck," Gnomeo admitted. His face had gotten wedged between two slats.

"So . . . can I see you again tomorrow?" he asked, his face slightly squished.

"Yes. But not here," she told him.

"Noon?" he asked hopefully.

"Not soon enough," she replied.

"I can do eleven-forty-five," he told her.

Juliet kissed her fingertips and placed them against Gnomeo's lips. Then, with a gentle push, she unstuck his head from the trellis.

"Back in the old deserted garden, then. Eleven-forty-five a.m.," Gnomeo called as he slipped down from the fence. "That frog was right. Parting is such sweet sorrow."

Juliet smiled. She was in love!

Gnomeo practically skipped into the Blue garden as he returned home with Shroom. But as soon as he shut the gate, Benny raced up to him.

"Gnomeo! Gnomeo! Where on earth have

you been, Gnomeo?" he cried frantically.

Gnomeo looked startled. "Well, I—"

"We thought one of those Reds must've gotten to you!" Benny exclaimed.

"A Red? Get to me? Yeah, as if," Gnomeo replied, shrugging uncomfortably. He thought of Juliet and sighed.

If Benny only knew.

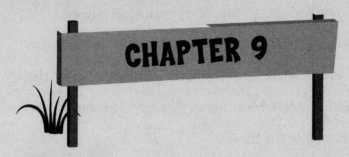

CHAPTER 9

The next day, Miss Montague walked out of her house bright and early. It was a beautiful day for gardening. "Ah la la la la ah," she sang as she made her way to the back shed.

As he stood on his pedestal, Gnomeo's eyes cut toward Miss Montague. She was about to discover what had happened to her lawn mower in the race with Tybalt.

Miss Montague unlatched the shed door and pulled out the mower. *Whumph!* All four wheels fell off the battered machine. *"Ahhhh!"* she cried in shock. She looked down at her ruined mower.

Gnomeo cringed.

In the Red garden, Mr. Capulet was also

recovering from an early-morning shock. He stood in front of his wishing well, which was covered with graffiti. He glared across the fence at Miss Montague. Clearly, she had to be responsible for this.

"This is an outrage!" he shouted. "The gardening gloves are off, then, are they?"

Miss Montague shook her finger at Mr. Capulet. "*You!* Wrecking my mower," she yelled back through the fence.

The two gardening rivals shouted back and forth at each other. This was war!

Miss Montague turned her back to Mr. Capulet and stormed toward her house. "Who thinks I should order the best new lawn mower my money can buy?" she growled as she slammed her back door.

A new lawn mower! Benny grinned. *Score!*

Later on in the Red garden, Tybalt, Fawn, and the Goons were busy scrubbing the graffiti from the wishing well.

"Why would anyone do this to Tybalt?" asked Fawn.

"Because nobody likes him!" replied one of the goons. Tybalt scowled.

"So, what are we going to do?" Fawn continued.

Tybalt's eyes wandered over the fence and rested on the Blues' prized wisteria. "Find their weak spot," he growled.

"*Then* what are we going to do?" Fawn asked. He was confused.

Tybalt laughed evilly. "Damage. Lots and lots of damage," he replied.

At the same time, in the Blue garden, Benny crept quietly up to Miss Montague's window. He peeked in and spotted her at her desk. She was browsing the Internet for a new lawn mower.

"Ohhh! She's on the worldy-widey-web!" Benny said gleefully.

Miss Montague scrolled through the lawn mower options. Each one was bigger and flashier than the last. There were so many possibilities to choose from!

Benny could hardly contain his excitement. "Yes," he whispered outside the window. "Pick that one! Oh, that one. I like that one, too!"

Then Miss Montague scrolled over a picture of the largest, glossiest, most high-tech lawn mower Benny had ever laid eyes on. This was the T. Rex of mowers: the Terrafirminator.

"Oh, what's this?" Miss Montague asked. She clicked on the Terrafirminator's picture.

A booming voice rang from the laptop. "Are you losing the war in your garden? Maybe it's

With the honor of the Blue garden at stake, Gnomeo pulls ahead of his rival, Tybalt, during a lawn mower race.

Fawn and the red-capped goons cheer when Tybalt wins the race by cheating.

Juliet prepares to sneak out of the Red garden with the help of her frog friend, Nanette.

Dressed for stealth, Juliet plans to take a beautiful orchid from an abandoned greenhouse.

Gnomeo and his best friend, Benny, slip into the Red garden. Luckily, Tybalt's goon doesn't recognize Benny in his disguise.

Gnomeo and Juliet fall in love when they meet. Unfortunately, he is a Blue, and she is a Red!

Nanette thinks Gnomeo and Juliet's romance
is wonderfully and tragically doomed!

Benny watches Miss Montague shopping online for a new lawn mower. He hopes she orders the powerful Terrafirminator!

Juliet and Nanette listen as a timid gnome named Paris sings to them.

Despite his love for Juliet, Gnomeo goes on a mission to spray pesticide on the Red garden's prized plants.

Tybalt and the goons spy on the Blue garden.

Tybalt tries to get rid of Gnomeo once and for all . . .

. . . and he appears to have succeeded!

This is war! The Blues prepare to avenge Gnomeo!

Gnomeo races back to the garden to save Juliet.

time for a secret weapon. *Terrafirminator!* It's the most ruthless five-hundred-horsepower grass-dominating piece of hardware the world has ever seen. It's unnecessarily powerful!"

Benny's eyes grew wide with admiration. "Ohhh, that one," he whispered. The Terra-firminator was perfect.

"Oh my!" Miss Montague exclaimed. She dragged the cursor toward the ordering box. Then she paused.

Benny watched in horror as Miss Montague moved the cursor toward a picture of a tiny pink mower instead.

"Oh, not the Kitten Clipper," Benny groaned.

Miss Montague clicked the BUY button.

Defeated, Benny slid down the wall onto the grass. Defeating the Reds with that tiny lawn mower would be next to impossible!

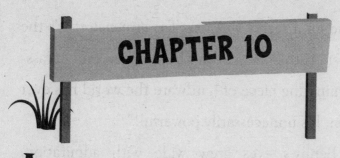

CHAPTER 10

At the same time that Gnomeo was on his way to meet Juliet, Nanette was busy helping Juliet make some finishing touches of her own. After a little sanding and buffing and a little drying with a leaf blower, Juliet looked lovelier than ever.

"Juliet!" Lord Redbrick suddenly called out. "There you are!"

Juliet looked over her shoulder to see her dad approaching. She bit her lip. Was it just her, or had her father been popping by at the most inconvenient times lately?

Lord Redbrick took his daughter by the arm and led her farther into the garden. Juliet looked back longingly at the garden gate. Nanette followed them. No way was she going to miss this.

"I've maybe misjudged your situation on that pedestal," Lord Redbrick announced. "It must be boring up there . . . and lonely. What you need is *companmanship*."

"Huh?" Juliet asked, startled.

"You know Paris, don't you?" Lord Redbrick continued, referring to a local gnome.

"Yes, yes, of course, why?" asked Juliet.

"Well, he's come to pay you a visit," her father announced, beaming with pleasure at his own cleverness.

Juliet, on the other hand, was not happy. "Dad!" she cried.

Lord Redbrick nudged Juliet around a corner. And there stood Paris, waiting for her. He adjusted his glasses nervously.

"Hello! Juliet! I've got something for you," Paris said as he shoved a bouquet of flowers in her direction. "Here. It's gypsophila. It means 'lover of chalk.'"

Juliet took the bouquet and sighed. She hated to be impolite, but she needed to end this conversation quickly or she would be late to meet Gnomeo. "Right . . . well, it's been nice speaking with you," she said. She hurried in the direction of the garden gate.

Paris scurried after her. "Where are you going?" he called, determined to see his courting of her to the end. He stepped in front of her. "But . . . um . . . surely it's a bit rude to leave me on our first date?"

Juliet raised an eyebrow. "First date?" she questioned.

"Yes," Paris replied. "And I thought, '*What does a boyfriend get his girlfriend?*'"

Boyfriend? Girlfriend? Juliet groaned at the thought of dating Paris.

Juliet was sure Paris was a nice, *dependable* gnome. But she had her heart set on someone else. Why couldn't her father just understand that she needed to live her own life?

Nanette giggled. "Oh, this is good!" she cried.

With a magician's *ta-da!* motion, Paris yanked a sheet off a large bush. The bush had been trimmed into the shape of the two of them dancing. "A small token of my affection," Paris declared. He grinned at Juliet.

"Oh, wow," Juliet mumbled, unsure of what to do. It was a nice gesture and all, but she was *not* about to be Paris's girlfriend!

"Juliet," Nanette said. "Do you realize what this is? It's a love triangle!"

Juliet moaned. A love triangle was not what she needed right now. What she needed was a way out of this mess!

Juliet motioned to Nanette with her eyes as

Paris began describing his creation in great detail. He was very excited about it.

Nanette nodded and slipped in close to Paris. As she listened, she began to see Paris in a different way. He was so passionate about his work! And so handsome!

It was now or never! As Nanette led Paris in the opposite direction, Juliet slipped out the back gate. She had a date to get to!

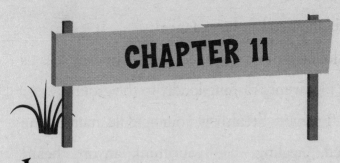

CHAPTER 11

Inside the deserted garden, Gnomeo gazed at his reflection in one of the windows of the greenhouse. For what must have been the tenth time, he practiced what he would say when Juliet arrived.

"Hey, Juliet! What a name—it goes with your eyes. Did it hurt when you fell down from heaven? So, how you doing?"

As Gnomeo was talking to himself, Juliet appeared in the reflection behind him. "Oh, I'm fine. How are you?" she said in a teasing voice.

Gnomeo spun around and blushed. *Busted!*

He leaned against a stack of firewood, trying to regain his cool. But the stack started to wobble and Gnomeo lost his balance!

Juliet pushed Gnomeo out of the way just as the logs went crashing loudly to the ground.

"I forgot. Stealth is your middle name," she joked, giggling. "Do you think anyone heard that?" she then wondered nervously.

"There's nobody here," Gnomeo replied. He smiled to himself. It was just the two of them. On a date. Together.

Juliet spotted something in the overgrown lawn nearby. She ran over and parted the long blades of grass in front of it.

"It's a 1950s model!" she cried. She couldn't believe it. This type of old-fashioned lawn mower was rare these days. "It's got the original chrome hubcaps!"

"Yeah, they featured those the first year," Gnomeo remarked, admiring the antique.

"Actually, they were available by special order

through 1954, when they switched to aluminum," Juliet corrected him, winking.

Gnomeo grinned. Not only was Juliet beautiful, but she also knew her mowers! She was too perfect.

"Let's start it up!" Juliet exclaimed.

Gnomeo hesitated, but only for a second. "Okay," he agreed. An opportunity like this was too good to pass up. He jumped on board and grabbed the throttle. "Check out the power on this beauty!"

He tried to start up the mower. *Putt, putt, putt.* He tried again. *Putt, putt.* Nothing. "She's empty," he said, disappointed. He looked around and spotted the old shed. There had to be some kind of fuel in there!

"Bingo," he said, taking Juliet by the hand.

Juliet found a long metal rod and offered it to Gnomeo. He used it to pick the lock on the shed door. The heavy door creaked as it opened.

The two gnomes crept inside the dark shed. As their eyes adjusted to the gloom, a gust of wind blew the door shut behind them. *Slam!* Gnomeo and Juliet jumped. Then, in the darkness, they heard an unfamiliar voice.

Gnomeo and Juliet screamed and scrambled to open the door. Racing into the yard, they dove behind the toppled pile of logs.

"What was that?" Gnomeo asked, panting.

"I have no idea," said Juliet. She eyed the shed door nervously.

Gnomeo took charge. "Okay," he called to the shed door. "Whatever you are, come out slowly. I have a loaded weapon and I'm not afraid to use it." He held the metal rod in his hand, ready to strike.

Gnomeo and Juliet waited. But nothing happened.

"Do you think I scared him?" Gnomeo asked Juliet.

"Oh, definitely," came a voice from behind them.

Gnomeo and Juliet shrieked again. *Who was that?*

"My name's Featherstone," said a plastic pink flamingo. Featherstone grabbed the metal rod Gnomeo was holding. He shoved it into the ground and perched on top of it. How nice to have his leg back!

Gnomeo looked relieved. Featherstone was a lawn ornament, just like them!

"Sorry, we didn't think anybody lived here!" Gnomeo told Featherstone.

But Juliet still looked nervous. She couldn't afford to be seen with Gnomeo. It was too risky.

"Yes, we shouldn't be here. We'll be going now," Juliet said nervously. She tugged on Gnomeo's sleeve, urging him to leave with her. The two took off across the grass.

But Featherstone wasn't going to let them get away easily. He was thrilled to have visitors, and besides, he'd recognized young love as soon as he'd seen them. "I think you two are on a date," he said knowingly.

Gnomeo and Juliet began talking at the same time, each trying to come up with a good cover story. "Date?" Gnomeo repeated. "Nooo. No, we're not—"

"Date? No way! What makes you think—?" Juliet started. "Definitely not dating—we're fighting. That's what we're doing."

"Yes," Gnomeo agreed. "Fighting to the death."

Juliet pointed at her hat and then at Gnomeo's. "Don't you see, we're mortal enemies," she said. "He's a Blue . . ."

"And she's a Red," Gnomeo finished.

Featherstone looked bored. "And I'm pink," he said with a shrug. Featherstone frankly didn't care why these two gnomes were in his garden. He was just glad to see *someone*. He had been locked in the shed alone for twenty years!

Featherstone looked sadly at the broken greenhouse windows and the scummy pond. He strode past Gnomeo and Juliet toward the old mower. He started to drag it across the overgrown grass.

"She's empty," Gnomeo told Featherstone.

"I've got gas in the shed," Featherstone replied. "It's in a can. Come on."

Gnomeo and Juliet beamed at each other. This was going to be *awesome*!

Within minutes the trio had the mower gassed up and ready to go.

"Let her rip," Gnomeo told Juliet, inviting her to start the old mower. A wide smile crossed her face as she pulled the throttle and revved the engine. Then she took off!

Juliet made some wild, sharp turns, almost flipping over, but she took each curve like a professional driver. After a few tricky, hair-raising moves around the old place, she screeched to a halt in front of Gnomeo and Featherstone.

"*Ta-da,*" Juliet announced as she leaped from the mower and landed in front of Gnomeo. When he looked at her path, he saw that she had carved the initials G+J into the tall grass.

"Fantastic penmanship," Featherstone said, admiring it. "But we still have to do something about these weeds."

"They're not weeds," Juliet said. "They're dandelion wishes. Go on. Make a wish and then blow on it."

"A weed by any other name . . . ," Featherstone replied sarcastically, before giving it a try. But his attempt at blowing on the dandelion didn't quite work. "It's kind of hard with a beak."

Then Featherstone tried one more time, and only one little white seed flew into the air. Featherstone sighed and walked away to be alone.

Juliet and Gnomeo looked at each other shyly and started to talk. Juliet decided to explain why her father was so strict.

"My dad's a little overprotective," Juliet admitted. In truth, driving the mower was the first unsafe thing she'd ever done—aside from sneaking around with Gnomeo.

Gnomeo understood exactly what Juliet was talking about. "Well, my mom raised me to hate you guys," he replied. "So it could never work. Could it?"

"A Red and a Blue," Juliet said sadly. "It just can't be."

Meanwhile, Featherstone had been blowing

dandelions successfully, and he wanted to make as many wishes as he could. "I wish we could all come back and do this tomorrow," he said. "I promise that your secret is safe with me."

Juliet looked at Gnomeo. It was as if Featherstone had read her mind.

"Should we?" Juliet asked Gnomeo.

"I can do eleven-forty-five," he said.

"Not soon enough," Juliet replied, giggling.

Gnomeo took Juliet's hand one last time, and then they parted.

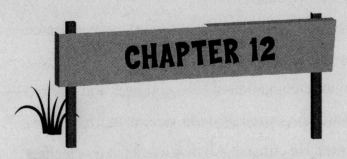

CHAPTER 12

Gnomeo walked through the Blue garden gate happily. He couldn't stop thinking about Juliet and their date. And he *really* couldn't wait to see her again tomorrow!

He was jarred out of his daydream when Shroom barreled into him. "*Ooofff!*" Gnomeo grunted.

Shroom was usually excited when Gnomeo came home, but this time he was acting a little crazy. Why was Shroom so anxious to see him? Gnomeo looked around for clues. When he saw the yard, his face fell.

Gnomeo spotted broken and cut pieces of

wisteria branches everywhere. They were scattered all over the lawn.

Gnomeo gathered his courage and looked toward the prized wisteria tree in its toilet bowl planter. He cringed. All that was left was a leafless bunch of broken sticks.

"Oh no," Gnomeo muttered. How could this have happened? He frantically looked around and finally saw his mother.

"How did it come to this?" Lady Bluebury sobbed from across the lawn. She sat on the ground and hugged one of the broken wisteria branches to her chest. "She was thriving so well this year," Lady Bluebury said sadly. "Struck down in full bloom!"

Gnomeo ran to his mother. "Mom!" he cried.

Lady Bluebury looked up at Gnomeo sternly. "Gnomeo! How could this have happened? Where were you?"

Gnomeo hung his head in shame. He had no excuse. The wisteria was ruined, and he had deserted his post in the garden. "I was—I was nowhere," he mumbled.

Lady Bluebury continued sobbing.

"Don't worry, Mom. I'll make it up to you," Gnomeo promised.

"How?" Lady Bluebury asked. "Redbrick and his hoodlums destroyed the most beautiful thing we Blues have. Your father and I planted her. We raised her from a seedling!"

Lady Bluebury ran across the lawn, crying. A group of small stone bunnies followed her.

Gnomeo didn't know what to do. He had never seen his mother so heartbroken before. And it was all his fault.

Benny held up a spray gun of weed killer. "Those blasted Reds! C'mon, Gnomeo, we'll make them pay!" he shouted, ready for revenge.

The crowd of Blues cheered. "Make 'em pay! Make 'em pay!" they chanted.

Benny thrust the weed killer into Gnomeo's hand. "Every last one of them!" Benny yelled, his fist raised into the air. It was a war cry.

Gnomeo looked at the spray gun in his hand and then at the chanting Blues. It was obvious what they wanted him to do. But he wasn't sure.

"Every last one," Gnomeo said, repeating Benny's words. But as he said it, he was thinking only of Juliet.

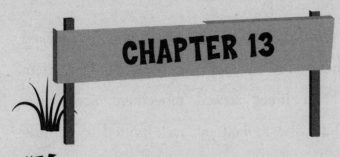

CHAPTER 13

"**M**y dad can really pick them," Juliet said to Nanette. They were listening to Paris serenading Juliet with a song he had written. Juliet was not impressed.

Nanette, on the other hand, had a dreamy look on her face. To her, Paris seemed like quite the catch!

Paris looked up as he sang his song to see Nanette gazing lovingly at him. He had never noticed how beautiful she was. He turned and sang in Nanette's direction this time. Love was certainly in the air!

Juliet giggled as she realized what was happening between Paris and her friend. She knew just how Nanette was feeling. She picked up her orchid and sniffed it, thinking of Gnomeo.

Then Juliet sensed movement across the garden. She looked up and spotted something tunneling underground by the fence. All of a sudden, Gnomeo popped out of the dirt.

Little did she know what was being planned by the Blues. Gnomeo had burrowed his way under the fence and had emerged in the Red garden, with Benny right behind him. Gnomeo was determined to set things right with his mother. And if that meant seeking revenge on the Reds, then so be it, even if he wasn't so sure about the plan.

Gnomeo took in his surroundings. Tybalt was with his goons, but they were too far away to notice Gnomeo and Benny. Gnomeo eyed the nearby tulips and crawled toward them. He aimed the spray gun of weed killer at the flowers. It was now or never.

Suddenly, Juliet sprang out in front of him—directly in his line of fire. Gnomeo jumped.

He must be here to surprise me, Juliet thought. She smiled. But then she noticed the spray bottle aimed at the tulips. It didn't take long for her to realize that this was not the kind of surprise she'd been hoping for. Her eyes darkened as she glared at Gnomeo. Then she stormed away silently.

"Juliet—no, wait!" Gnomeo called after her. This wasn't his idea. He didn't even really want to do it.

But Juliet had disappeared.

A hippo lawn ornament spotted Gnome. "A Blue! A Blue!" it began to shout.

Gnomeo shot back into the tunnel he had dug. Benny quickly followed, but not before Tybalt was able to catch a glimpse of him.

Tybalt ran up to the fence and put his eye to a small hole. He quickly realized what the Blues had been up to and, looking at Benny, said to himself, "Such a big hat for such a small brain."

He turned to Fawn and the goons, who were right behind him. "So, you boys fancy a little bit of fun?" He walked toward his mower. "Let's take this baby out into the alley," he said.

As usual, Fawn was slow to catch on. "*Then* what are we going to do?" he asked.

"We're going to have a *smashing* good time!" Tybalt gave a sinister laugh. "*Ah-hahaha!*" He revved his mower, and the goons cheered.

The Reds were ready to strike again.

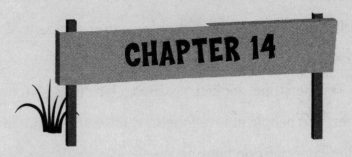

CHAPTER 14

Later that afternoon, Gnomeo tracked down Juliet in Featherstone's garden. He tried to explain himself, but Juliet wasn't in the mood to listen.

"Is that your big move on a second date? Wine them, dine them, and then spray them with weed killer?" she asked. She was still angry.

"Well, you have to admit, it *is* original," Gnomeo said sheepishly.

Featherstone spotted them from across the garden and walked over. "Are you back already?" he asked, delighted to see them.

Gnomeo and Juliet ignored him and continued to argue.

"Juliet, be reasonable," Gnomeo pleaded

with her. "I didn't have a choice after Incident Wisteria."

Featherstone looked worried. He hated it when two people in love fought. But Gnomeo and Juliet kept right on fighting.

Featherstone tried one more time. "Come on, guys, can't we just all laugh about this?"

Juliet and Gnomeo looked at him sharply.

"We're in the middle of something—do you mind?" Gnomeo snapped.

"You wouldn't understand, all right?" Juliet added. "So just leave us alone."

Featherstone looked upset. He was only trying to help. "Oh. Sorry. Sometimes I get a little overexcited . . . especially having such great new friends," he said. "I know I can be a bit much." He sadly walked away.

Gnomeo and Juliet looked at each other guiltily. Poor Featherstone. This wasn't his fault.

"Wait, Featherstone," Gnomeo called after him. He hadn't meant to hurt his feelings.

"Come back! We're sorry!" Juliet pleaded.

But Featherstone wasn't in the garden anymore.

Gnomeo and Juliet went to the shed to find him. When they walked through the door, their mouths dropped open.

Featherstone's home was beautiful! One whole wall was decorated with pictures and memorabilia that Featherstone had collected over the years. Gnomeo and Juliet looked more closely and noticed one photograph in particular. It was worn around the edges and showed the same garden long ago, tidy and in full bloom. In the background stood *two* pink flamingos.

Featherstone came up behind them. He looked at the picture and said, "I understand more than you think. I was in love once, too."

Looking off into the distance, Featherstone walked toward the greenhouse.

Gnomeo and Juliet followed him.

Featherstone told them about his past. Long ago, a young couple had lived in this house. They took care of the garden and were wonderfully in love. Featherstone was in love, too—with another pink flamingo the couple had planted on the lawn. It was such a happy time for them all. Featherstone thought it would last forever.

But then the couple's love simply died, and they decided to part ways. They sold their house and abandoned their garden. Featherstone's girlfriend was packed away in a moving van. And Featherstone was locked in the shed. He had never seen his girlfriend again, though he thought about her every day.

Featherstone sighed, heartbroken. He missed her now just as much as he had all those years ago.

Gnomeo looked at Juliet. Suddenly, he felt scared. What if the same thing happened to him and Juliet? What if they never saw each other again? Gnomeo had to make sure that would never happen.

Gnomeo clasped Juliet's hands. "What if we never went back?" he suggested.

Juliet frowned and said, "Never go back? But what about my dad and Nanette and the Red garden?" Juliet loved Gnomeo with all her heart. But could she really leave the rest of her world behind? She wasn't sure.

"See, the truth is, over there we're enemies. But over here"—Gnomeo spread his arms wide— "we're a matching pair."

He smiled at the thought of always being with Juliet.

Juliet looked deep into Gnomeo's eyes. She couldn't imagine life without him.

"Juliet," Gnomeo said. "Will you stay here and build a garden with me?"

"I would love to," Juliet replied. She felt like the luckiest girl in the world.

Featherstone beamed. He loved a happy ending!

Gnomeo and Juliet leaned in to kiss. It was the perfect moment. But suddenly, they heard a loud noise.

Bang! Bang! Bang!

Benny was slamming the greenhouse window with his fists. Benny looked horrified. His best friend was about to kiss a Red! "Gnomeo!" he shouted through the glass. "What are you doing?"

Gnomeo stammered, "B-Benny, listen. I—I can explain."

But it was too late. Distraught, Benny had run away.

Benny burst into the alleyway, out of breath. His head was spinning. *What was Gnomeo thinking?* Benny was so distracted that he wasn't even looking where he was going. He ran smack into Tybalt and the goons.

Tybalt sat on his mower with his arms crossed. "Well, well, well. If it isn't little big-hat Benny," he sneered. He revved his lawn mower's engine.

Uh-oh, Benny thought. He looked around for an escape route.

"Mess with our garden, will ya?" Tybalt asked. His eyes narrowed. He had a shovel in his hand and began twirling it menacingly.

Benny spied the open gate of the Blue garden only a few feet away. Could he make it in time?

Just then, Gnomeo and Shroom ran into the alleyway. Gnomeo took in the scene.

"Benny!" he called.

Tybalt swung his shovel in the air. *Swish!* He

sliced it straight through the top of Benny's hat.

"No!" Gnomeo cried.

Benny fell backward. He felt the area where his hat used to be. It was gone. "Oh no!" he cried helplessly.

"Oh, that felt good," Tybalt said.

Gnomeo's face darkened. He couldn't let Tybalt get away with this. "Tybalt!" Gnomeo thundered.

Tybalt gunned his mower's engine and drove straight toward Gnomeo.

A snarling Gnomeo grabbed a nearby pipe and jumped onto the moving mower.

Juliet ran out of the garden and saw Gnomeo and Tybalt sparring. "No!" she cried.

As the mower sped down the alleyway, Gnomeo and Tybalt crashed their weapons together. *Clash! Clash! Clang! Clang!*

Gnomeo easily sent Tybalt's shovel flying.

"You wouldn't attack an unarmed gnome, would you?" Tybalt asked.

Gnomeo knew he could destroy Tybalt right then and there. But he was too honorable to keep fighting with a weapon when his opponent was unarmed. He flung his pipe away and put up his fists.

But Tybalt wasn't one to fight fair. He pushed a lever on his mower. The mower shuddered, making Gnomeo lose his balance.

"Sucker!" Tybalt taunted.

Still off balance, Gnomeo was leaning precariously over the side of the mower. Tybalt pushed Gnomeo's head dangerously close to the ground. Gnomeo had nowhere to go! He looked up for a split second and realized they were speeding toward big trouble.

"Tybalt! The wall!" he yelled.

"You think I'm going to fall for that old trick?

Ha!" Tybalt called over the roar of the mower.

Gnomeo shoved Tybalt away from him just in time. He dove off the mower, landing safely on a patch of grass.

Tybalt looked up. His face dropped when he realized he was about to crash.

The lawn mower smashed into the wall. When the dust cleared, everyone could see that Tybalt had crumbled into a million pieces.

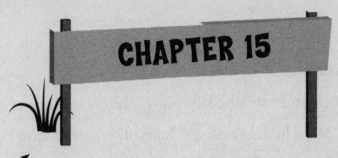

CHAPTER 15

Inside both gardens, Lord Redbrick and Lady Bluebury heard a terrible sound.

"What was that?" Lord Redbrick asked.

"What's happened?" asked Lady Bluebury.

They rushed through their back gates. A crowd of Reds and Blues poured into the alley to see what the commotion was about.

Fawn and the goons had circled Gnomeo. Gnomeo had destroyed their leader, and now they were going to crush him. "Smash him back!" one of the goons yelled.

Juliet ran in front of Gnomeo, protecting him. "No!" she cried.

Lord Redbrick held up his arms to quiet

the crowd. "What is the meaning of all this constipation?" he asked.

"Gnomeo smashed Tybalt—" the goons began.

"No! He didn't do it!" Juliet interrupted. She wasn't going to let Gnomeo take the blame for something he hadn't done.

Lord Redbrick looked confused. Why was Juliet protecting a Blue? He turned to his daughter. "Juliet?" he asked.

Lady Bluebury cocked her head. "Gnomeo?" she questioned.

But the goons didn't care about explanations. They were hungry for revenge. "A gnome for a gnome!" they shouted, pelting Gnomeo with pebbles and rubble.

"Run, Gnomeo, run!" Juliet called.

Gnomeo took off down the alley, toward the street. A gang of angry Reds followed him.

Lady Bluebury ran after the mob. "Stop! Stop that!" she shouted.

A crowd of Blues burst into the alleyway and chased after the Reds. This was all-out war!

Gnomeo reached the end of the alley. The street beyond only led to the dangerous outside world. He was trapped. The angry mob closed in on him. He squeezed his eyes shut and waited.

Then someone came jogging down the street. The gnomes were forced to freeze. The human jogger turned down the alley, but when she saw all the gnomes, she slowed down. "Creepy," she muttered as she took a different route—but not before she had accidentally knocked Gnomeo into the road.

A speeding car raced down the street. Its tire clipped Gnomeo, sending him flying into the intersection.

Juliet ran toward him, but Lord Redbrick grabbed her. "What are you doing?" he demanded.

"I love him!" cried Juliet.

The crowd gasped.

Lord Redbrick looked stunned. "What?" he asked in disbelief.

Suddenly, a delivery truck appeared. It was headed straight for Gnomeo. After it had passed by, Gnomeo was gone! And in his place was nothing but a blue pile of crushed ceramic.

"No!" Juliet screamed, tying to rush out into the street.

"There has been enough smashing for one day. Get back on your pedestal!" Lord Redbrick shouted.

Juliet struggled to break free, but the Reds dragged her away.

"My poor boy," Lady Bluebury sobbed as the Blues led her back into their garden.

Only Shroom remained in the alley. He hopped into the middle of the street. The little mushroom nudged the pile of ceramic pieces and discovered that they were only the remains of a blue teapot. Shroom looked down the street and saw that Gnomeo was alive and hanging on to the grille of the truck. When it came to a stop, Gnomeo hopped off—only to be swept up in the slobbering jaws of a bulldog!

Shroom watched as the bulldog disappeared around the corner with Gnomeo.

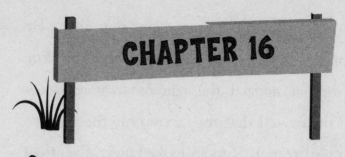

CHAPTER 16

Gnomeo was getting a grand tour of Stratford-Upon-Avon, traveling all over town in the bulldog's mouth. He wondered where he would end up.

The dog stopped suddenly and dropped Gnomeo. He dug a hole to bury his new toy.

Gnomeo saw his chance for escape. He rolled away from the dog's drooly jaws. Then he hopped into a nearby drainpipe.

Gnomeo walked along the inside of the pipe. When he came out the other end, he found himself under a bench in the middle of an open park.

But no sooner had Gnomeo taken a few steps

out from under the bench than he spotted a group of teenagers strolling by. They scooped up the little gnome and carried him away.

"Looks like your sister," one of the boys said to another. The teenagers laughed and tossed Gnomeo back and forth between them like a football. They ran toward the middle of the park.

Now what? Gnomeo wondered.

Back in the Red Garden, two gnomes were trying to wrestle Juliet onto her pedestal.

"You've left me no choice," Lord Redbrick told Juliet. "I lost your mother, and I am not going to lose you."

With a nod from Lord Redbrick, the goons secured Juliet to her pedestal with heavy-duty superglue.

Stuck in place, Juliet felt her eyes fill with

tears. If only her father would listen to her, she could explain. Didn't he know what it was like to be in love? She gazed over the fence toward the greenhouse. She could just see the stem of another orchid starting to grow through the roof.

She wept for all the things that might have been.

Juliet wasn't the only one upset by the day's events.

In the Blue garden, Lady Bluebury wiped a tear from her eye. She thought of Gnomeo and the terrible fact that she would never see him again. But she sobbed all over again when she saw the bunnies holding up a wreath that spelled out GNOMEO.

Featherstone was gloomy and alone again. Seeing two young people in love being torn apart reminded him of his own loss. If only there were something he could do.

While each side mourned its loss, Benny was scheming. He would show those Reds once and for all. He huddled with the stone bunnies to give them the details. Pointing to Miss Montague's house, he made some sketches in the dirt with a stick. He had a plan.

Shroom tried to get Benny's attention to let him know that Gnomeo was alive but needed their help. But Benny was too busy plotting to destroy the Red garden to notice Shroom.

The small stone mushroom darted across the alley in search of Featherstone. Someone had to help him find Gnomeo before it was too late!

Benny and the stone bunnies crept under Miss Montague's window. They peered inside to make sure the laptop computer was still on her desk.

Benny weaved his way back through the garden and jumped into a drainage pipe. He walked through the pipe, which ended inside Miss Montague's washing machine. From there, he made his way to the laptop.

The Kitten Clipper order flashed on the screen. Benny tapped some keys with his foot and danced across the touch pad to cancel the purchase. Next he found the high-powered lawn-crushing machine called the Terrafirminator. Benny danced on the keys and ordered it with one-hour rush delivery!

The bunnies tapped on the window. Miss Montague had returned home unexpectedly. Thinking quickly, Benny disguised himself as a doll on her shelf.

As soon as Miss Montague had left the room, Benny slipped out. Phase one of his mission was now complete.

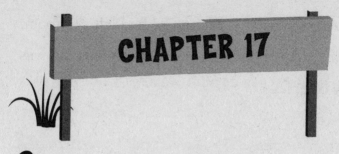

CHAPTER 17

Back in the park, the teenagers had left Gnomeo on top of a statue of William Shakespeare.

This is my weirdest destination yet, Gnomeo thought as he looked down at the statue of the famous writer. But he made the most of it by telling William Shakespeare (Bill for short) his story. He spared no detail, from his first meeting with Juliet to the final duel with Tybalt.

Bill listened carefully, taking it all in. "Extraordinary, your story," he said, thinking of a famous play he had once written. "It does put me in mind of another."

"It does?" Gnomeo asked. *How on earth could there be another story like mine?*

"Oh, indeed," replied Bill. "Yes, there are *remarkable* similarities."

Gnomeo was hopeful. Maybe this other story could shed some light on his current situation. "What happens? Do they get back together?" he asked.

Bill thought for a moment. "Not exactly," he said, finally deciding that he should tell the little gnome the grim truth. "The girl feigns her death. The boy finds her and thinks she is dead. Takes his own life. She wakes. Finds him dead. Takes her life. Both dead. The end."

Bill became so excited as he retold the story that Gnomeo slipped from his head. Luckily, Gnomeo managed to grab hold of the writing quill in Bill's hand.

"They both die?" Gnomeo asked as he dangled from the tip of the quill. He shot Bill a determined look. "There's got to be a better ending than that!"

That's just what they said, Bill thought, gesturing with the quill in his hand as he remembered the two characters from his play. The sudden movement made Gnomeo lose his grip.

Bill gasped as Gnomeo fell toward the ground and certain doom.

Gnomeo held his breath as he fell, waiting to shatter on the concrete below. But instead of hitting the hard ground, Gnomeo landed on Featherstone!

"Featherstone!" Gnomeo shouted with joy as he looked down at his friend. Gnomeo hoped he hadn't hurt Featherstone!

"One word," Featherstone said, taking a deep breath and popping himself back into shape. "Plastic!"

"How did you find me?" Gnomeo asked.

Shroom leaped into Gnomeo's arms, squirming like an excited puppy.

"He sniffed you out," Featherstone said.

"I knew I could count on you," Gnomeo told Shroom as the little mushroom continued to gesture as wildly as he could. "What's that? Juliet is in danger? I've got to get back!"

Gnomeo and his friends didn't waste any time heading back to the gardens. The statue of William Shakespeare watched the three would-be heroes exit the park on their mission to save Juliet.

"It will end in tragedy," Bill said, shaking his head.

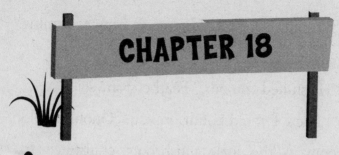

CHAPTER 18

On the other side of town, Benny heard a delivery truck pull into Miss Montague's driveway. He rubbed his hands together gleefully.

He ran to the driveway and gazed up at the machine. "Ohhhh," he breathed. *What a beauty!*

Benny climbed aboard the mower as a crowd of Blues came to admire it. Benny sat in the seat and raised his arms in a V for victory. The crowd cheered.

Lady Bluebury stepped through the crowd. "Benny?" she asked.

"What do you think, Lady B? This baby is fully equipped," Benny said.

Lady Bluebury looked worried. "Equipped for what?" she asked.

"It has settings for edging, trimming, mulching, and *revenge*!" Benny replied, his eyes wild.

Lady Bluebury looked toward the fence. She wanted those Reds to pay for what they had done to her Gnomeo. "Do it, Benny," she growled. "Do anything it takes. Make them rue the day they destroyed my son."

The gnomes cheered again. Lady Bluebury looked up at Benny proudly and declared, "Unleash the dogs of war!"

Benny pressed the Terrafirminator's START button. The engine roared to life like a tiger and then settled into a deadly purr. The computerized weapon of destruction counted down to one, then lurched into action. A camera popped out of the dashboard and scanned the yard. It locked on to its target: the fence separating the gardens.

Benny switched gears and barreled toward the fence.

The Terrafirminator ripped through the fence. As it entered the Red garden, Benny let out a mighty battle cry. *"Raaaaah!"*

The goons and dozens of Reds leaped out of the Terrafirminator's path.

The mower fixed its sights on the red boat planter and demolished it. Reds ran screaming around the garden.

Lord Redbrick winced.

Juliet, Nanette, and Paris watched in horror as Benny's mechanical beast destroyed their home. And after that, it headed right for the wishing well!

"Yes!" Benny hooted. He was getting revenge for Gnomeo—and it felt *good!* He was so wrapped up in the moment that he lost control of the machine.

The Terrafirminator switched directions and took aim at the Blue garden. It smashed into the prized toilet planter and got stuck. The impact sent Benny flying.

With the pause in the action, Lord Redbrick came to his senses. "Attack!" he commanded the Reds.

"Counterattack!" shouted Lady Bluebury to the Blues.

The gnomes rushed at each other from both sides. For missiles, they threw fresh garden produce. Soon every gnome was covered in sticky crushed berries and crimson tomato juice. Everyone fought, and no one was safe.

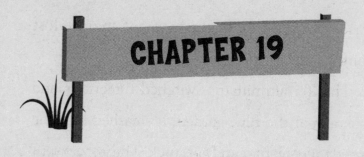

CHAPTER 19

Gnomeo and Shroom rode on Featherstone's back as the long-legged bird raced along the streets of Stratford-Upon-Avon. Taking a shortcut and avoiding humans, they zoomed through town, leaping over anything in their way. They finally reached the alley on Verona Drive, but Featherstone's legs became stuck in a trash bag. Exhausted and out of breath, he waved for Gnomeo to go on without him.

Gnomeo scaled the fence and jumped on top of the Red garden shed. But he did not expect the sight below.

The gardens were a war zone. Gnomes fighting

gnomes, shrubbery destroyed, and flowers cut down in full bloom. It was total chaos.

Gnomeo spotted Juliet. The crowd swirled around her. "Juliet!" he called out to her.

Juliet looked up at him and gasped. "Gnomeo, you're alive!" she cried with relief.

She wanted to run to him, but she was still glued to her pedestal.

Gnomeo had to save her! But before he could act, a tomato smacked him in the face. He lost his balance and tumbled from the roof. He landed in the pond below.

"No! No!" Juliet shouted above the noise.

The mob of Red gnomes pelted Gnomeo with berries. He struggled to climb out of the pond.

Meanwhile, a stray berry hit the Terrafirminator's control panel, setting it to COMPLETE DESTRUCTION mode. The terrifying mower revved as it powered up to break free. Its computerized targeting system was homing in on its next objective—Juliet's pedestal!

"It's going to blow!" Benny shouted.

The Terrafirminator suddenly launched itself into the air. The gnomes stopped fighting and watched as it flew over their heads.

Gnomeo tried to free Juliet, but the glue was just too strong.

Lord Redbrick saw his daughter in danger. "No!" he shouted.

"My son!" Lady Bluebury gasped.

Everyone turned to see Gnomeo and Juliet. They were doomed! *Doomed!*

Bill Shakespeare was right, Gnomeo thought. *This is it!*

With no way out, Gnomeo looked deeply into Juliet's eyes.

"It's no use," Juliet insisted. *"Go!"*

"I'm not going anywhere," Gnomeo told her. As the shadow of the Terrafirminator loomed over them, Gnomeo and Juliet looked at each other sadly. Their love was just not meant to be.

KA-BOOM! The Terrafirminator slammed into Juliet's grotto and exploded. A huge, billowing cloud of black smoke rose above the houses on Verona Drive.

Then all was quiet.

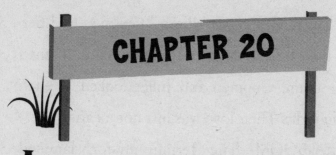

CHAPTER 20

As the dust settled, Red and Blue gnomes pulled themselves out of the wreckage. They looked around at what had once been the two most beautiful gardens in town. Both were now completely destroyed.

Paris crawled out of the rubble. He and Nanette helped each other to their feet. She had rescued his glasses and now placed them on his nose.

Featherstone, who had finally reached the garden, searched for his two friends. His metal legs trembled under him as he lost hope.

Benny pulled Shroom from a pile of rocks.

Shroom ran to where Juliet's pedestal had been, looking for Gnomeo. He sniffed for any sign of survivors. Then he shook his head sadly.

Lady Bluebury and Lord Redbrick joined Shroom. They looked at the grotto, now just a pile of rubble.

"No," Lord Redbrick said softly. Lady Bluebury closed her eyes.

They hung their heads in shame. How had things gotten so out of control?

"I'm sorry about your son," Lord Redbrick said.

"I'm sorry about your daughter," Lady Bluebury sobbed.

Lord Redbrick stretched out his hand to Lady Bluebury and said, "This feud . . ."

". . . is over," Lady Bluebury finished. The feud, which had started off as a playful rivalry, had cost them far too much.

As they shook hands, Lord Redbrick accidentally stepped on the switch that operated Juliet's mechanized grotto. Some of the rubble at the top of the grotto shifted just a bit. The water began to spray, moving even more rocks.

Lord Redbrick pushed Lady Bluebury out of the way of a falling stone. Lord Redbrick and Lady Bluebury raised their heads as loud music began to play and lights twinkled through the debris. Juliet's musical grotto rotated up through the rubble.

Then a hand appeared! Could it be?

Gnomeo emerged. He reached down and pulled Juliet up.

They were alive!

Gnomeo and Juliet looked down, and all the gnomes, Red and Blue, began to cheer.

"I don't know about you," Gnomeo said, taking Juliet in his arms, "but I think this ending is *much* better."

Juliet smiled gratefully. She was happy that she and Gnomeo had survived!

And all the gnomes were relieved as well. The Reds and Blues began to dance, while Gnomeo and Juliet smiled at each other happily. The gardens might have been ruined, but true love was alive and in full bloom.

In the park, Bill Shakespeare smiled. He had to admit it: Some people—and some gnomes—just deserved a happy ending.